eco-antics

BY
MABEL A. HAMMERSMITH
AND LAURA WATKINS

ILLUSTRATED BY BEVERLY ARMSTRONG

SPECIAL THANKS TO ELAINE ROMINE, HEIDI HUGHES, AND BILL NIXON.

ECO-ANTICS WAS PRODUCED BY GIRL SCOUTS OF THE U.S.A.
FRANCINE T.R. CRAVEN, DIRECTOR, PROGRAM DEPARTMENT
VINCENT YANNIE, SENIOR DESIGNER
MICHAEL CHANWICK, ART DIRECTOR
SYLVIA FEINMAN, EDITOR
CAROLYN CAGGINE, PUBLICATIONS MANAGER

PRODUCED DURING THE TENURE OF DR. CECILY C. SELBY,
NATIONAL EXECUTIVE DIRECTOR.

ISBN 0-88441-132-X

MY NAME IS ______________________

I LIVE IN A
CITY CALLED ______________________

MY ADDRESS IS

____

THERE ARE ________ PEOPLE
LIVING IN MY CITY.

THINGS I LIKE BEST ABOUT MY
CITY ARE:

____

____

____

____

THINGS I DON'T LIKE ABOUT IT ARE:

____

____

____

____

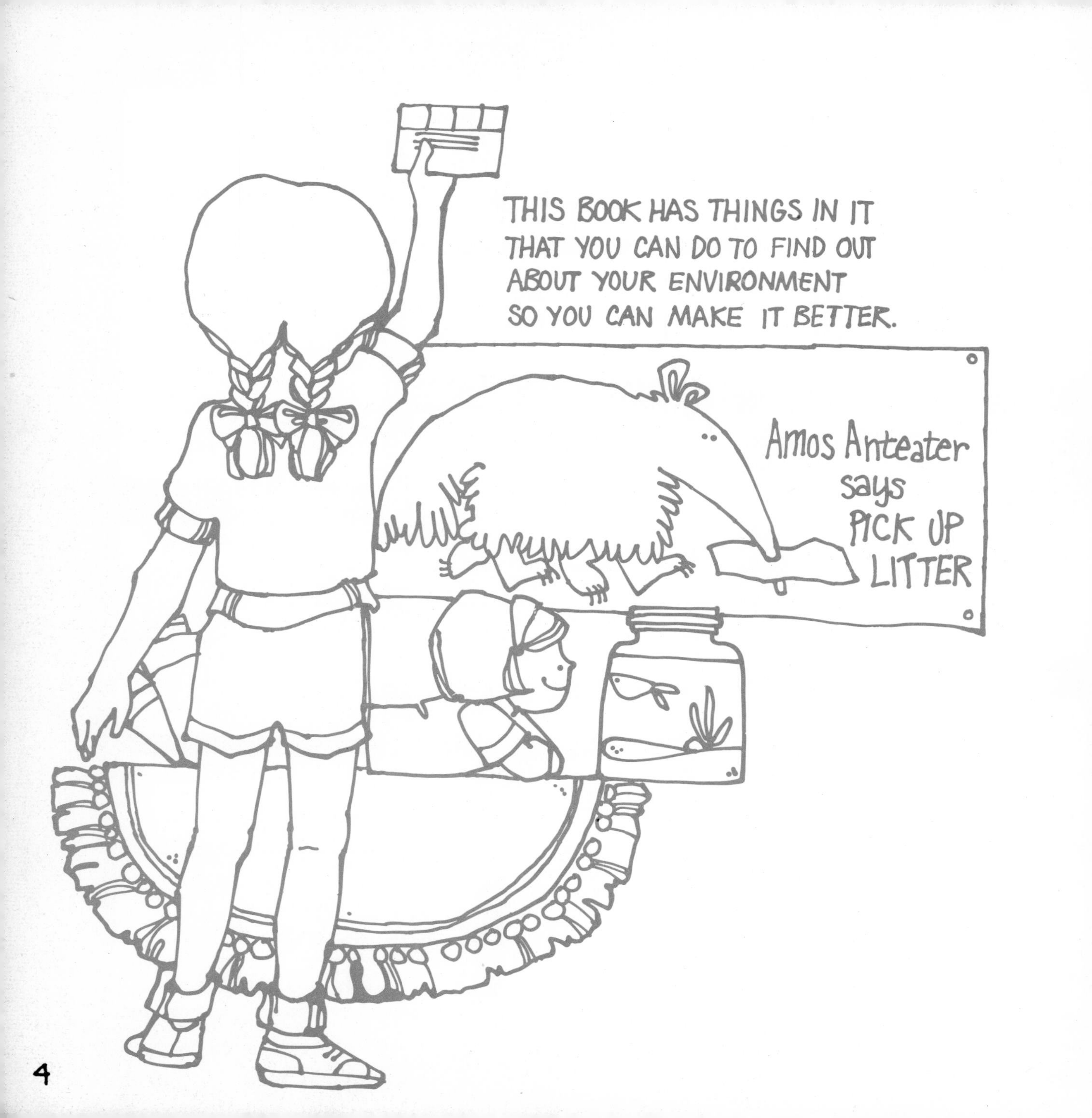
THIS BOOK HAS THINGS IN IT
THAT YOU CAN DO TO FIND OUT
ABOUT YOUR ENVIRONMENT
SO YOU CAN MAKE IT BETTER.
Amos Anteater
says
PICK UP
LITTER

PEOPLE IN ANY CITY NEED

BUILD THE KIND OF CITY YOU WOULD LIKE TO LIVE IN. YOU CAN MAKE IT OUT OF MANY THINGS: BOXES, CANS, BRICKS, BOARDS, AND ANYTHING ELSE YOU CAN FIND. WHAT WILL YOU NAME YOUR CITY?

WOULD YOU LIKE TO LIVE ON THIS STREET? DRAW A PICTURE OF THE STREET WHERE YOU LIVE. WHAT IS SPECIAL ABOUT YOUR STREET? WHAT IS NOT SO NICE? WHAT WOULD YOU LIKE TO CHANGE?

DID YOUR STREET ALWAYS LOOK THIS WAY? SEE IF YOU CAN FIND MAPS AND PICTURES OF THE WAY IT USED TO BE.

DID YOU EVER WATCH A BUILDING GOING UP?

WHAT DO YOU SEE WHEN YOU WALK BY A CONSTRUCTION SITE?
WHAT DO YOU HEAR?
WHAT ARE THE WORKERS DOING?
WHAT TOOLS DO THEY USE?
WHAT THINGS GO INTO MAKING A BUILDING?

MY STORY OF A BUILDING GOING UP

DRAW A PICTURE STORY OF A BUILDING GOING UP. DATE THE PICTURES.
WHEN THE BUILDING IS FINISHED LOOK AT ALL YOUR PICTURES.
CAN YOU TELL OTHER PEOPLE WHAT HAPPENED IN EACH PICTURE?

1
2
3
4

MAKE PICTURES EVERY DAY OR TWO AND DATE THEM. DO YOU THINK IT IS EASIER TO BUILD A BUILDING OR TO TEAR ONE DOWN?

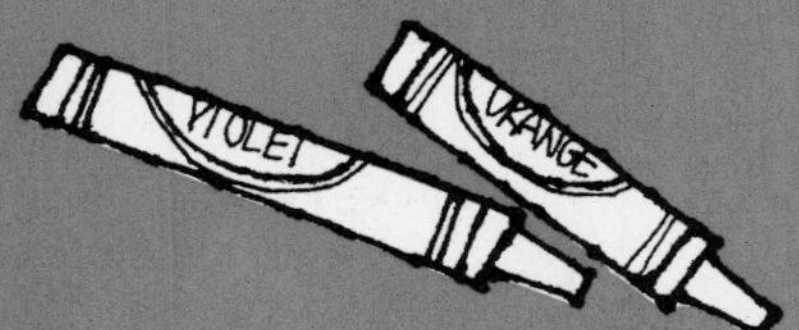

DRAW A PICTURE OF WHAT YOU WOULD LIKE TO SEE IN THE PLACE WHERE THE BUILDING WAS.

HOW MUCH SPACE DO YOU NEED?

HOW MANY PEOPLE LIVE ON YOUR BLOCK? HOW MANY LIVED THERE FIVE YEARS AGO? HOW MANY DO YOU THINK WILL LIVE THERE FIVE YEARS FROM NOW?

DRAW HOMES FOR FOUR FAMILIES IN ONE BOX. NOW DRAW HOMES FOR TWENTY-FIVE FAMILIES IN THE OTHER BOX.
WHAT DID YOU HAVE TO DO? HOW DID THE HOMES CHANGE?

WHAT HAPPENS TO A PLACE WHEN MORE PEOPLE LIVE THERE?

DO YOU REALLY SEE? YOUR ENVIRONMENT IS EVERYTHING AROUND YOU. IT IS LIVING THINGS AND NON-LIVING THINGS. HOW MANY LIVING THINGS CAN YOU FIND IN THIS PICTURE ? WHAT DO THEY NEED IN ORDER TO LIVE ? TAKE A CLOSE LOOK AT YOUR OWN ENVIRONMENT. WHO SHARES IT WITH YOU ?

A FOREST COMMUNITY

IS LIKE YOUR COMMUNITY, WITH MANY PLANTS AND ANIMALS LIVING TOGETHER. IN THIS PICTURE, CAN YOU FIND THINGS THAT SEEM LIKE:

APARTMENTS
TRAFFIC
A BASEMENT
PLUMBING
A STOREHOUSE
A GARBAGE DISPOSAL

WATCH ANTS BUILD THEIR OWN CITY

FIRST BUILD AN ANT HOUSE AND THEN COLLECT SOME ANTS. (BE SURE TO TAKE ALL THE ANTS FROM ONE SPOT.) PUT THEM IN THE ANT HOUSE. FEED THEM FOOD CRUMBS AND GRASS EACH WEEK.

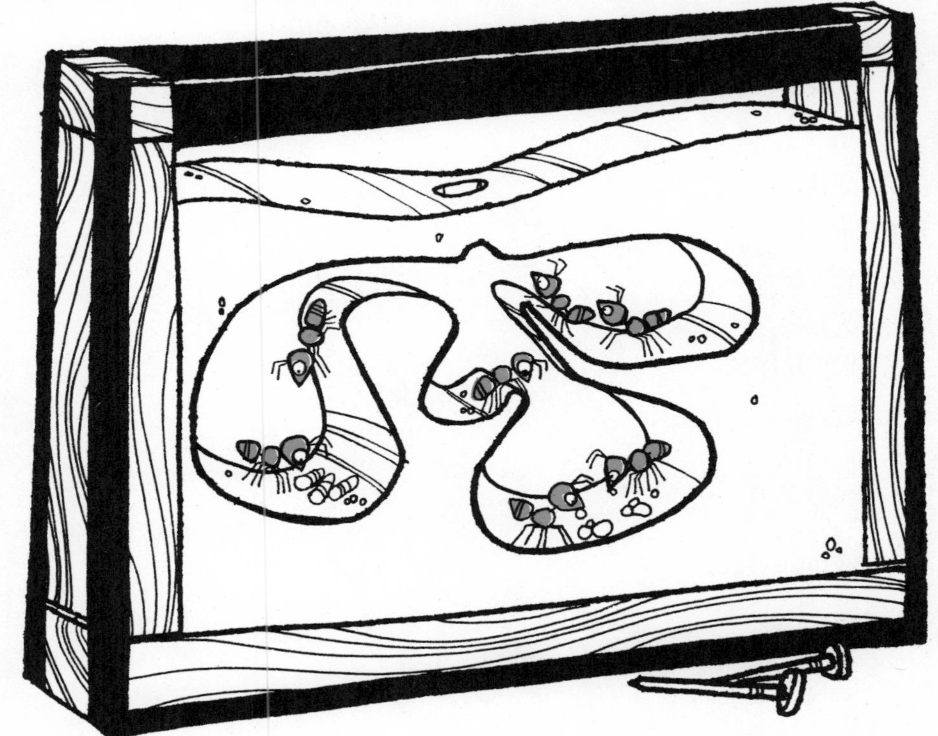

TO BUILD AN ANT HOUSE YOU WILL NEED: TWO PIECES OF GLASS OR PLASTIC THE SAME SIZE, ONE LONG PIECE OF 1"×1" WOOD, A ROLL OF STRONG TAPE, A HAMMER, NAILS, A SAW, AND ENOUGH DIRT TO FILL YOUR ANT HOUSE HALF-WAY.

1. CUT TWO PIECES OF WOOD THE LENGTH OF THE GLASS.
2. CUT TWO MORE PIECES OF WOOD TO FIT BETWEEN THE LONG ONES.
3. NAIL THE TWO SHORT PIECES TO ONE OF THE LONG ONES.
4. USE STRONG TAPE TO ATTACH THE GLASS TO THE WOOD. ADD DIRT HALF-WAY TO THE TOP. PUT IN THE ANTS AND TAPE THE FOURTH PIECE ON TOP AS THE LID.

A POND IS A DIFFERENT ENVIRONMENT.
HAVE YOU EVER EXPLORED A POND?
WHAT DID YOU SEE THERE?
HOW MANY LIVING THINGS CAN YOU FIND IN THE PICTURE?
MINNOW • TURTLE • TADPOLE • CATTAIL • KINGFISHER • GARTER SNAKE • DUCKWEED
DRAGONFLY • SNAIL • WATER STRIDER • GIANT WATER BUG

HAVE A RUB-IN

WHAT DOES YOUR ENVIRONMENT FEEL LIKE? YOU CAN SEE WHAT IT FEELS LIKE BY MAKING A RUBBING.

1. PUT A PIECE OF PAPER OVER WHAT YOU ARE GOING TO RUB.
2. RUB A CRAYON GENTLY OVER THE PAPER.
3. SEE WHAT IT FEELS LIKE.

EVERY LIVING THING NEEDS WATER

DO YOU KNOW WHERE THE WATER YOU USE COMES FROM AND WHAT HAPPENS TO IT AFTER IT IS USED?

WATER FALLS UPON THE EARTH AS RAIN, HAIL, OR SNOW.

IT SINKS INTO THE DIRT OR RUNS OFF THE SURFACE INTO SWAMPS, RIVERS, LAKES, AND SEWERS FROM WHICH IT FINALLY REACHES THE SEA.

SOIL WATER MAY ALSO DRAIN BY WAY OF SPRINGS INTO LAKES, RIVERS, AND THE SEA.

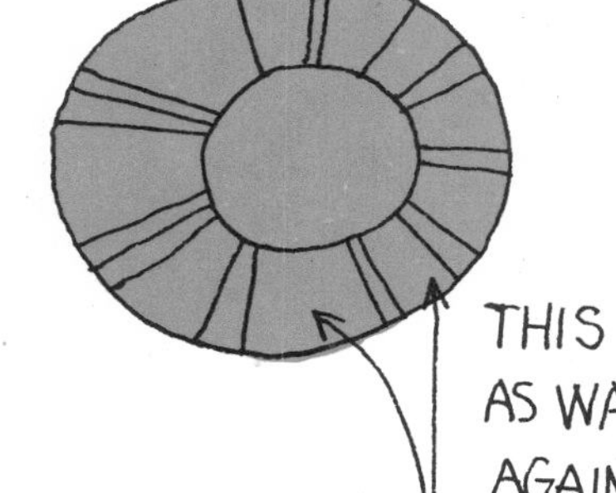

THIS WATER GOES INTO THE AIR AS WATER VAPOR UNTIL IT FALLS AGAIN AS RAIN, HAIL, OR SNOW.

WATER IS ALSO EVAPORATED DIRECTLY FROM THE SURFACE OF THE LAND AND BODIES OF WATER.

MUCH WATER IS TAKEN FROM THE SOIL BY PLANTS. THIS WATER, CARRYING OXYGEN, HYDROGEN, AND MINERALS, TRAVELS UP THE STEM AND EVAPORATES INTO THE AIR THROUGH THE LEAVES.

CAN YOU FOLLOW A RAINDROP IN THIS PICTURE?

HOW MANY KINDS OF POLLUTION DO YOU SEE?
WHAT DO YOU THINK POLLUTION DOES TO THE RAINDROP?

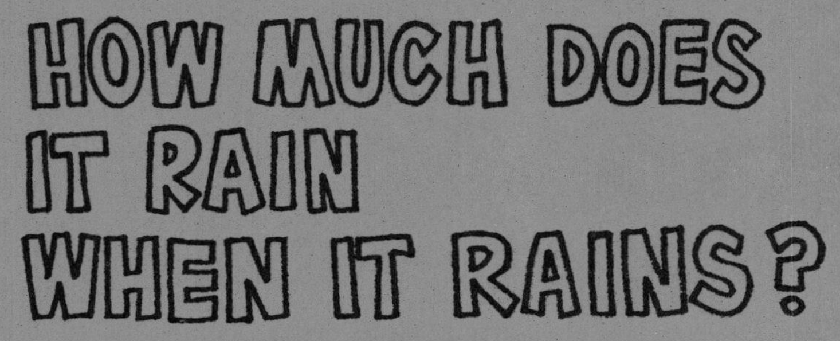

HOW MUCH DOES IT RAIN WHEN IT RAINS?

ONE WAY YOU CAN FIND OUT IS TO MAKE A RAIN GAUGE. TAKE A LARGE TIN CAN. STAND A RULER UP IN IT SO THE END WITH THE NUMBER 1 RESTS ON THE BOTTOM. PUT THE CAN ON THE GROUND WHERE IT WILL CATCH THE RAIN. AFTER A RAIN STORM, SEE HOW MUCH RAIN HAS FALLEN. CHECK WITH THE NEWSPAPER. DID THEY FIND THAT THE SAME AMOUNT OF RAIN HAD FALLEN? KEEP TRACK OF THE RAINFALL FOR A MONTH.

DID YOU EVER

CATCH A SNOWFLAKE?

A SNOWFLAKE BEGINS HIGH ABOVE THE EARTH WHEN WATER VAPOR FREEZES AROUND A TINY DUST PARTICLE. THE SNOWFLAKE TURNS AND SPINS AS IT FALLS, FORMING MANY DIFFERENT SHAPES. NO TWO SNOWFLAKES ARE ALIKE.

SNOW AND ICE ARE IMPORTANT TO OUR ENVIRONMENT. SNOW BECOMES A WARM BLANKET FOR THE EARTH. SOIL DOES NOT FREEZE SO HARD UNDER SNOW. MANY ANIMALS AND PLANTS WOULD DIE IN WINTER WITHOUT THIS BLANKET.

YOU CAN KEEP A SNOWFLAKE. PUT A PIECE OF GLASS AND A CAN OF CLEAR LACQUER SPRAY INTO THE FREEZER FOR A FEW MOMENTS. THEN TAKE THEM OUTDOORS BEFORE THEY HAVE TIME TO WARM UP. SPRAY A THIN COAT OF LACQUER ON THE GLASS AND HOLD IT SO SNOW WILL FALL ON IT. THEN PLACE THE GLASS UNDER COVER IN A COLD PLACE. LEAVE IT THERE FOR FIFTEEN MINUTES. THE LACQUER WILL REPLACE THE SNOWFLAKE AND WILL BE WHITE. NOW YOU CAN KEEP THE SNOWFLAKE AND LOOK AT IT THROUGH A MAGNIFYING GLASS.

HOW WARM IS IT TODAY?
IF YOU HAVE A CRICKET IN YOUR HOUSE, THE CRICKET CAN HELP YOU TO TELL THE TEMPERATURE. THIS IS HOW TO DO IT: COUNT THE NUMBER OF CHIRPS IT MAKES IN 15 SECONDS. ADD 40. THE RESULT WILL BE THE TEMPERATURE WHERE THE CRICKET IS LOCATED. CRICKETS MAKE THEIR CHIRPING SOUND BY RAISING THEIR WINGS STRAIGHT UP AND RUBBING THEM AGAINST EACH OTHER. THE HOTTER THE WEATHER, THE FASTER THEY CHIRP.

TAKE A CLOSER LOOK

YOU CAN MAKE THINGS LOOK BIGGER BY MAGNIFYING THEM. A BOTTLE FULL OF WATER MAGNIFIES. AND SO DO THE BOTTOMS OF SOME DRINKING GLASSES.

EVEN A DROP OF WATER MAGNIFIES

CUT OUT THE CENTER OF A PIECE OF CARDBOARD.

TAPE A PIECE OF CLEAR PLASTIC OVER THE HOLE.

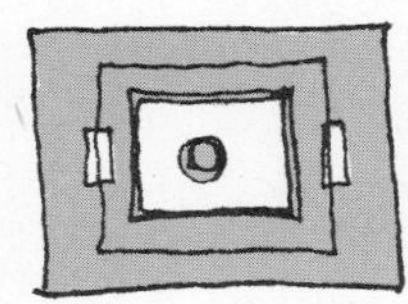

ADD A DROP OF WATER AND LOOK THROUGH IT AT YOUR HAND.

TAKE A CLOSER LOOK AT SOMETHING IN YOUR ENVIRONMENT.

FOOD CHAINS

ALL LIVING THINGS ARE PART OF A FOOD CHAIN. SOME ARE CALLED PRODUCERS. SOME ARE CALLED CONSUMERS. SOME ARE CALLED DECOMPOSERS.

GREEN PLANTS ARE PRODUCERS. THEY ARE THE ONLY LIVING THINGS THAT CAN CHANGE ENERGY FROM THE SUN, AIR, WATER, AND MINERALS IN THE GROUND INTO FOOD.

OTHER LIVING THINGS ARE CONSUMERS. THEY EAT THE SEEDS, FRUITS, BARK, LEAVES, AND ROOTS MANUFACTURED BY THE GREEN PLANTS.

SOME CONSUMERS BECOME FOOD FOR OTHER LIVING THINGS. ANIMALS THAT EAT OTHER ANIMALS ARE ALSO CONSUMERS.

BACTERIA, MILLIPEDES, EARTHWORMS, AND FUNGI ARE DECOMPOSERS. THEY GET NOURISHMENT FROM DEAD AND DECAYING THINGS.

CONSUMERS AND DECOMPOSERS BOTH LEAVE BEHIND WASTE PRODUCTS WHICH ENRICH THE SOIL AND HELP PLANTS TO GROW.

HOW MANY FOOD CHAINS CAN YOU FIND IN THIS PICTURE? REMEMBER THAT SOME LIVING THINGS FIT INTO MANY FOOD CHAINS. DRAW LINES BETWEEN THE PARTS OF EACH CHAIN.

THE SPIDER-WEB PATTERN FORMED WHEN THESE LINES CROSS IS CALLED THE WEB OF LIFE. WHAT HAPPENS TO THE PICTURE WHEN ONE ANIMAL'S FOOD SUPPLY IS MISSING?

POLLUTION

IS ANYTHING THAT
SPOILS THE ENVIRONMENT

HOW MANY KINDS OF AIR POLLUTION CAN YOU FIND IN THIS PICTURE?

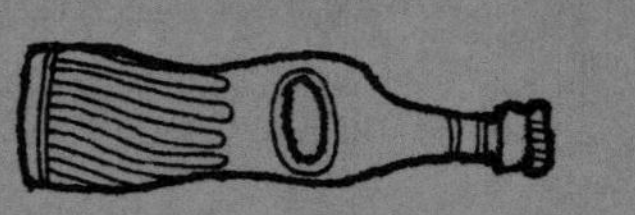

HERE'S A TONGUE TWISTER FOR YOU:

DEPOSITABLE BOTTLE.

TRY IT!

HOW POLLUTED IS THE AIR? FIND OUT.

EXPERIMENT 1

YOU WILL NEED SOME WHITE CARDS, VASELINE, AND MASKING TAPE.

1. SPREAD VASELINE ON EACH CARD.
2. TAPE CARDS IN DIFFERENT PLACES INDOORS AND OUTDOORS.
3. LOOK AT THEM EACH DAY FOR THREE OR FOUR DAYS. WHERE IS THE AIR THE DIRTIEST?

EXPERIMENT 2

YOU WILL NEED AN OLD NYLON STOCKING, TWO SHOE BOX COVERS (OR PIECES OF CARDBOARD ABOUT THAT SIZE), AND SCISSORS.

1. CUT THE NYLON STOCKING INTO TWO PIECES.
2. STRETCH EACH PIECE OVER A CARDBOARD.

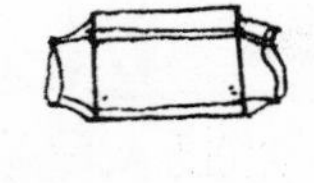

3. KEEP ONE IN A CLOSET AND PUT THE OTHER OUTSIDE.
4. LOOK AT THEM IN A FEW WEEKS. WHICH PIECE OF NYLON WAS MOST DAMAGED BY THE AIR?

EXPERIMENT 3

1.	2.	3.	4.

YOU CAN USE THE SHADED SQUARES ABOVE TO SEE HOW DIRTY THE AIR IS. KEEP A RECORD OF THE POLLUTION THAT YOU SEE

- COMING OUT OF A CHIMNEY
- FROM A JET PLANE'S EXHAUST AFTER TAKEOFF
- OVER A PARK

EXPERIMENT 4

YOU WILL NEED SOME RUBBER BANDS AND TWO PIECES OF WOOD (TWO RULERS ARE GOOD).

1. STRETCH TWO RUBBER BANDS OVER EACH RULER.
2. PUT ONE IN A CLOSET AND ONE OUTDOORS.
3. LOOK AT THEM AGAIN IN A FEW WEEKS. WHAT HAPPENS TO THE RUBBER BANDS IF THE AIR IS POLLUTED?

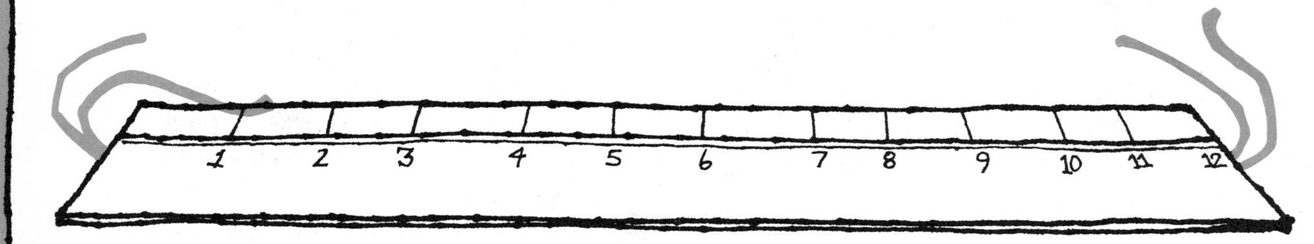

MAKE A CLOCK

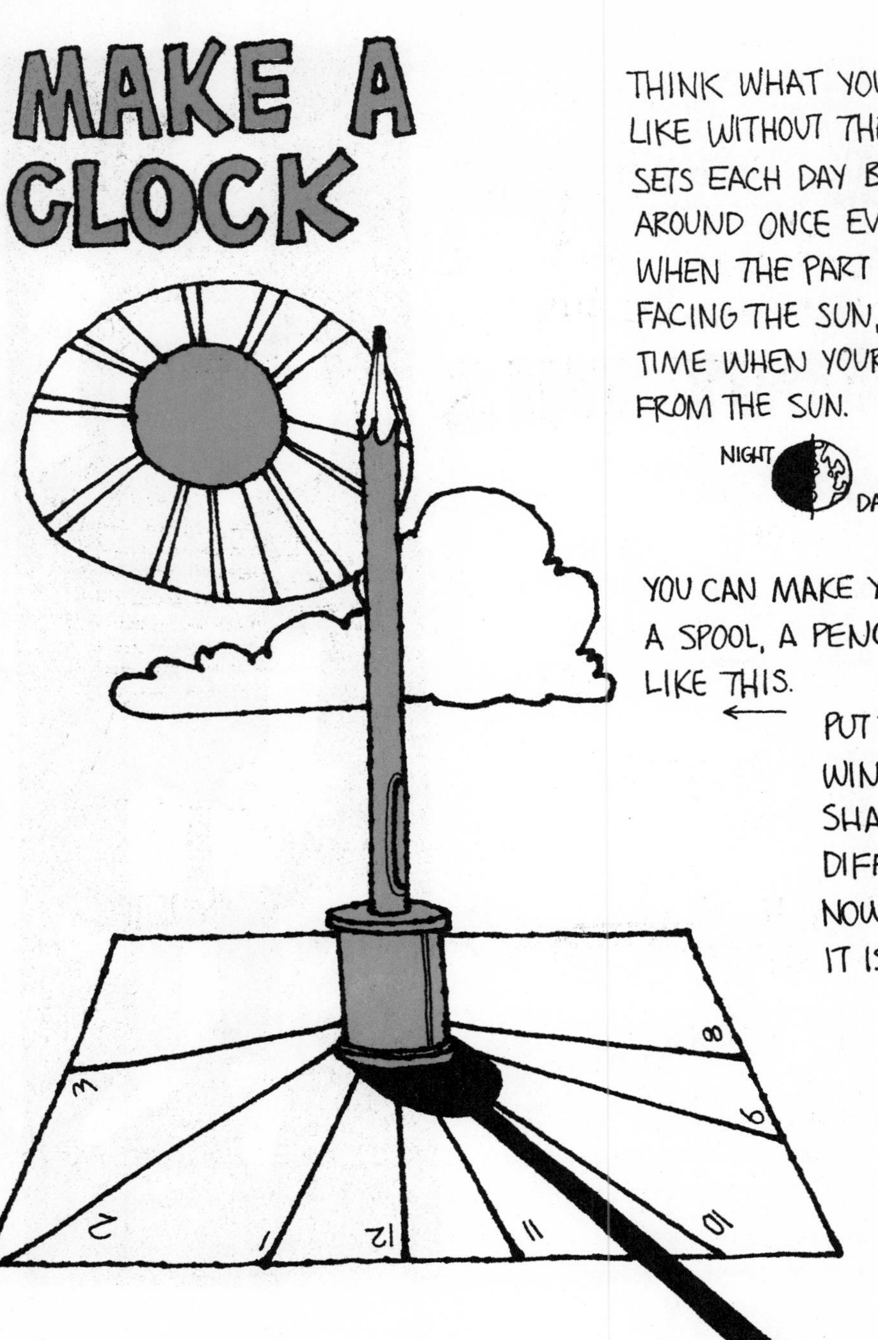

THINK WHAT YOUR ENVIRONMENT WOULD BE LIKE WITHOUT THE SUN! THE SUN RISES AND SETS EACH DAY BECAUSE THE EARTH SPINS AROUND ONCE EVERY TWENTY-FOUR HOURS. WHEN THE PART OF THE WORLD YOU ARE IN IS FACING THE SUN, IT IS DAYTIME. IT IS NIGHT-TIME WHEN YOUR PART OF THE WORLD IS AWAY FROM THE SUN.

NIGHT DAY SUN

YOU CAN MAKE YOUR OWN SUN-CLOCK OUT OF A SPOOL, A PENCIL, AND A PIECE OF PAPER, LIKE THIS. ←

PUT THEM ON A SUNNY WINDOWSILL AND TRACE THE SHADOW THE PENCIL MAKES AT DIFFERENT TIMES OF THE DAY. NOW YOU CAN TELL WHAT TIME IT IS WITH YOUR SUN-CLOCK.

EACH TIME YOU TURN ON A LIGHT YOU ARE HELPING TO POLLUTE THE EVIRONMENT AND USE UP OUR NATURAL RESOURCES.

THINK ABOUT THIS

ELECTRIC POWER IS PRODUCED BY

1. FUEL-POWERED GENERATORS
   - CONSUME LIMITED FUEL (OIL, COAL, GAS).
   - RELEASE POLLUTANTS INTO THE AIR.
2. WATER-POWERED HYDROELECTRIC PLANTS
   - USE WATER POWER.
   - CAUSE THERMAL (HEAT) POLLUTION.
   - DAMS CHANGE ECOSYSTEM.
3. NUCLEAR REACTORS
   - CAUSE THERMAL POLLUTION AND POSSIBLY RADIATION CONTAMINATION.

WHAT CAN YOU DO TO SAVE NATURAL RESOURCES AND STOP POLLUTING?

HOW DOES YOUR FAMILY RATE AS GOOD ELECTRICITY USERS?

		DO YOU KEEP LIGHTS OFF WHEN THEY ARE NOT NEEDED?
ON OFF		DO YOU TURN OFF THE TV AND RADIO WHEN YOU ARE NOT LOOKING OR LISTENING?
		DO YOU TURN OFF AIR-CONDITIONERS, FANS, OR EXTRA HEATERS WHEN NO ONE IS AT HOME?
		DO YOU USE MAJOR APPLIANCES BEFORE 8 A.M. OR AFTER 6 P.M.?
		DO YOU KEEP RADIATORS UNCOVERED AND WINDOW SHADES UP ON COLD DAYS?
		DO YOU KEEP THE SUN OUT ON HOT DAYS?

IF YOU ANSWERED YES TO ALL SIX QUESTIONS, YOU ARE GOOD ELECTRICITY USERS. CONGRATULATIONS!

DO YOU REALLY NEED THAT APPLIANCE?

LOOK AT THE LIST OF APPLIANCES AND THE AMOUNT OF ELECTRICITY THEY USE.

APPLIANCE	AVERAGE WATTS PER HOUR
ROOM AIR-CONDITIONER	1,566
CAN OPENER	1.2
CLOCK	2
COFFEE MAKER	894
FAN (COOLING)	88
TV (COLOR)	332
TV (BLACK AND WHITE)	237
FROSTLESS REFRIGERATOR-FREEZER	615
REFRIGERATOR-FREEZER	326
TOASTER	1,146
RADIO	71
DISHWASHER	1,201
VACUUM CLEANER	630
HAND IRON	1,088

WHAT APPLIANCES DO YOU HAVE IN YOUR HOUSE? WHICH ONES CAN YOU DO WITHOUT? MAKE A LIST OF THE ONES YOU USED TODAY AND WHY YOU USED THEM.

Appliance	Why Used
can opener	open can of cat food
toothbrush	brush teeth

HOW MUCH ELECTRICAL POWER COULD YOUR FAMILY SAVE?

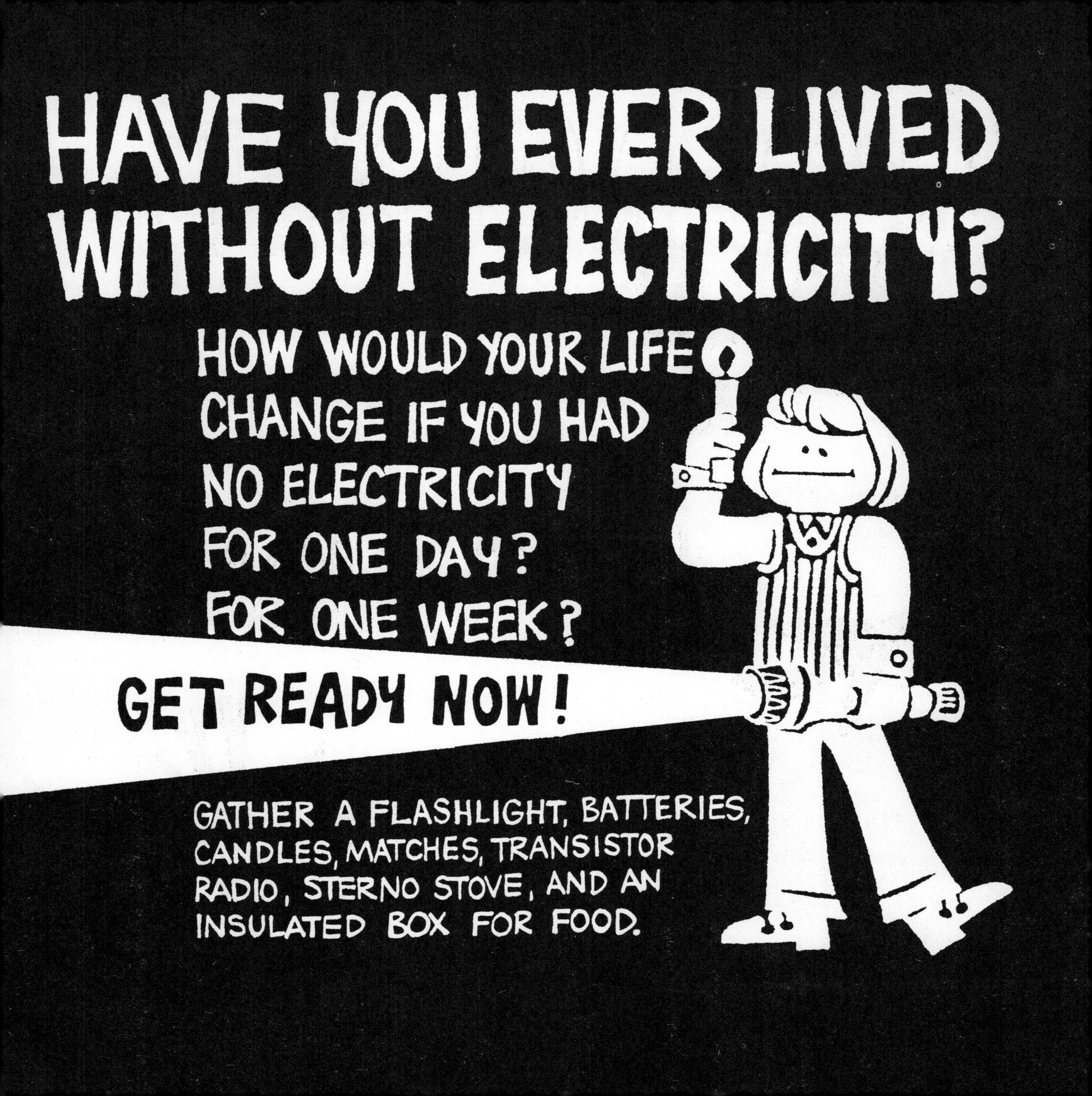

HAVE YOU EVER LIVED WITHOUT ELECTRICITY?

HOW WOULD YOUR LIFE
CHANGE IF YOU HAD
NO ELECTRICITY
FOR ONE DAY?
FOR ONE WEEK?

GET READY NOW!

GATHER A FLASHLIGHT, BATTERIES,
CANDLES, MATCHES, TRANSISTOR
RADIO, STERNO STOVE, AND AN
INSULATED BOX FOR FOOD.

NOISE!

SOME SOUNDS ARE NICE.

OTHER SOUNDS ARE NOT SO NICE.

NOISE IS MEASURED IN DECIBELS. WHEN A JET TAKES OFF, IT MAKES

1,000,000,000,000,000

TIMES AS MUCH NOISE AS THE RUSTLING OF A LEAF.

DID YOU KNOW THAT SOUNDS OVER 90 DECIBELS CAN HURT YOUR EARS?

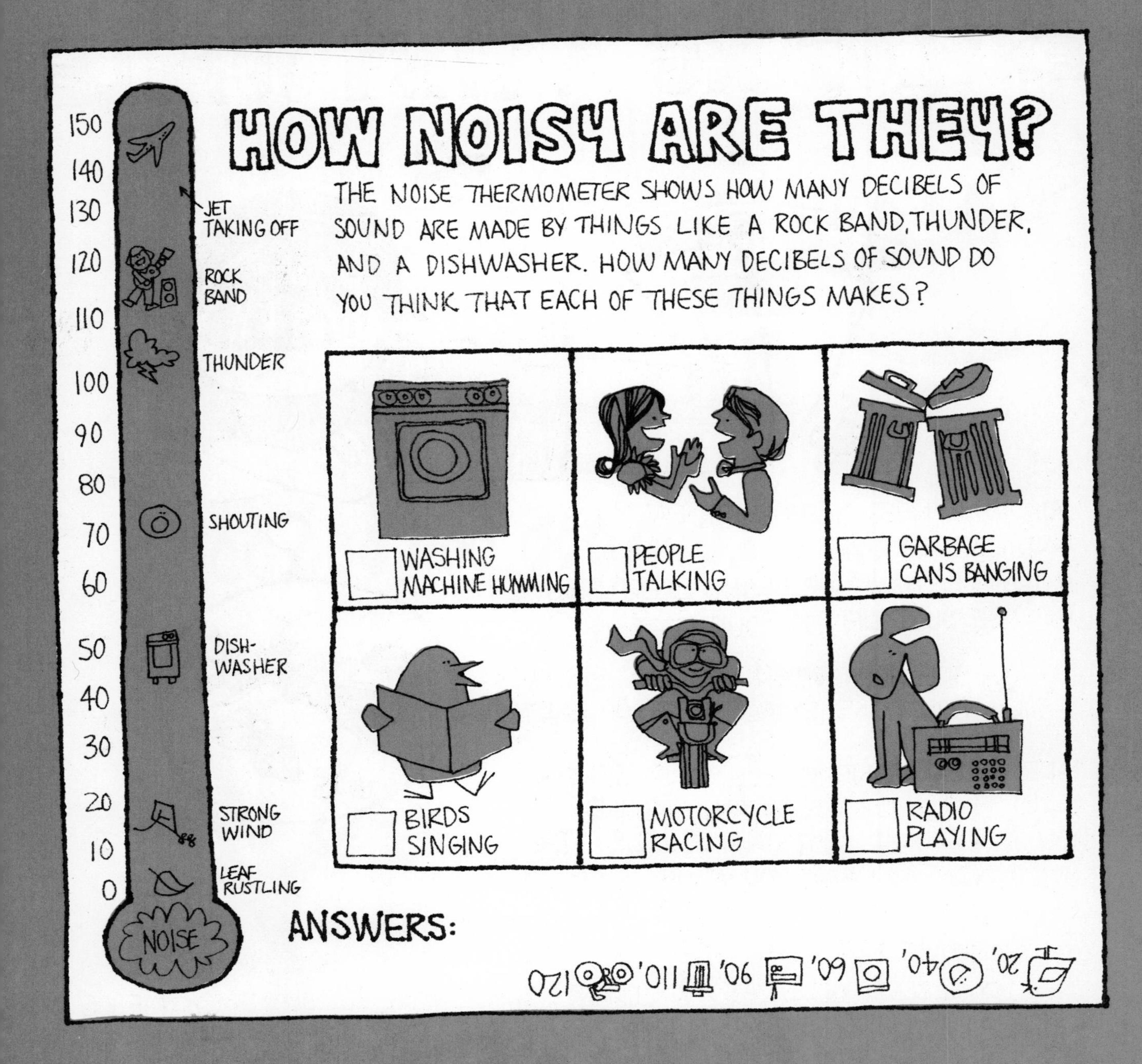
HOW NOISY ARE THEY?
THE NOISE THERMOMETER SHOWS HOW MANY DECIBELS OF SOUND ARE MADE BY THINGS LIKE A ROCK BAND, THUNDER, AND A DISHWASHER. HOW MANY DECIBELS OF SOUND DO YOU THINK THAT EACH OF THESE THINGS MAKES?
150
140
130
120
110
100
90
80
70
60
50
40
30
20
10
0
JET TAKING OFF
ROCK BAND
THUNDER
SHOUTING
DISH-WASHER
STRONG WIND
LEAF RUSTLING
NOISE
WASHING MACHINE HUMMING
PEOPLE TALKING
GARBAGE CANS BANGING
BIRDS SINGING
MOTORCYCLE RACING
RADIO PLAYING
ANSWERS:
20, 40, 60, 90, 110, 120

EXPLORING A TINY JUNGLE

YOU WILL NEED YOUR EYES, EARS, NOSE, AND LOTS OF TIME.
A WHOLE TOWN OF LIVING CREATURES MAY BE JUST UNDER YOUR FEET.

SEE HOW MUCH YOU CAN DISCOVER ABOUT ONE SMALL PIECE OF EARTH.

TAKE A COAT HANGER AND BEND IT. PLACE IT DOWN ON THE GROUND. EXPLORE JUST WHAT IS INSIDE THE COAT HANGER. YOU MIGHT FIND

MAKE YOUR OWN INDOOR JUNGLE

A BIG GLASS JAR CAN HOUSE A MINI-ECOSYSTEM.
PUT IN SOME ROCKS AND PEBBLES AND SAND.
THEN ADD A LAYER OF DIRT.
NOW YOU CAN PLANT SEEDS OR GROWING PLANTS IN THE DIRT.
YOU MAY WANT TO ADD AN INSECT OR TWO.
IF YOU SEAL YOUR TINY JUNGLE WITH PLASTIC OR A LID,
YOU CAN WATCH THE RAINDROP CYCLE HAPPENING INSIDE IT.

TRAIN A FISH

IMAGINE HOW AMAZED YOUR FRIENDS WILL BE WHEN YOU HOLD UP A CARD THAT SAYS "COME TO THE SURFACE" AND YOUR FISH DOES! HERE'S HOW: BUY A GOLDFISH AND KEEP IT IN A BIG BOTTLE OR TANK THAT HOLDS AT LEAST A GALLON OF WATER. BUY A BOX OF FISH FOOD, TOO. FOLLOW THE DIRECTIONS FOR FEEDING ON THE BOX. HOLD THE CARD NEXT TO THE TANK AS YOU FEED YOUR FISH. TAKE IT AWAY WHEN THE FISH HAS FINISHED EATING. IN A FEW DAYS, YOUR FISH WILL COME TO THE SURFACE WHENEVER YOU BRING THE CARD NEAR.

SPY ON A FLY

HERE'S HOW: GET A JAR. PUNCH HOLES IN THE LID WITH A NAIL SO THE FLY CAN BREATHE. CATCH A FLY IF YOU CAN. HINT– WAIT FOR THE FLY TO BUZZ INTO A WINDOW. THEN GENTLY GRAB IT WITH YOUR HAND AND PUT IT IN THE JAR. AFTER YOU PUT THE LID ON, WASH YOUR HANDS. NOW YOU CAN GET A CLOSER LOOK AT YOUR FLY. HOW MANY LEGS DOES IT HAVE? HOW ARE ITS LEGS DIFFERENT FROM YOURS? WHAT COLOR IS IT? MIX SOME SUGAR IN WATER AND GIVE YOUR FLY ONE DROP OF SUGAR WATER A DAY. WATCH IT EAT. HOW IS THE FLY'S MOUTH DIFFERENT FROM YOURS? ITS EYES?

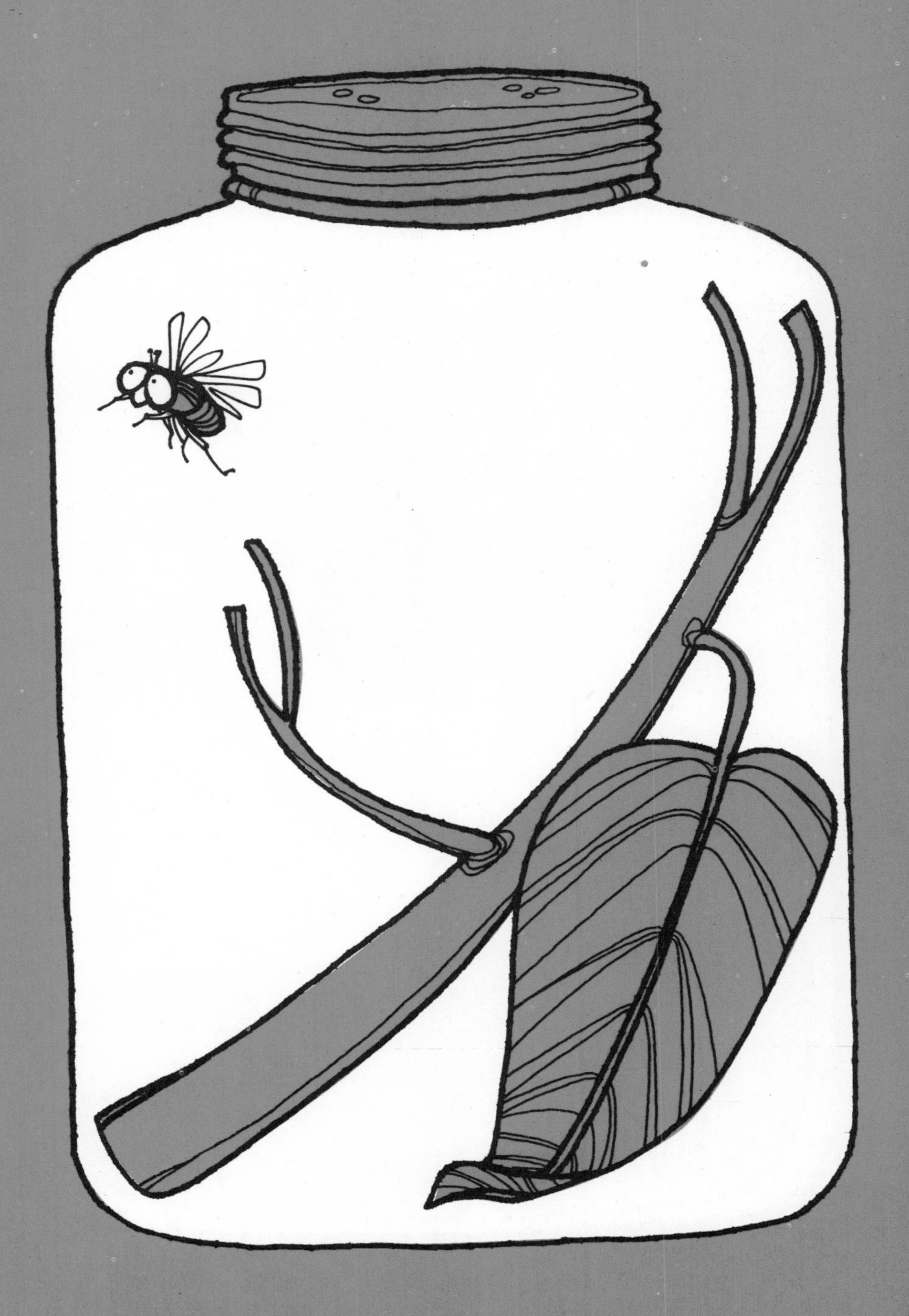

WHAT'S A TREE TO YOU?

MAKE FRIENDS WITH A TREE.
FIND A TREE YOU LIKE.
MAKE PICTURES OF IT IN THE
SUMMER, FALL, WINTER, AND SPRING.
WHO LIVES IN YOUR TREE?

THE KINDS OF BUTTERFLIES YOU HAVE IN YOUR NEIGHBORHOOD WILL DEPEND ON THE KINDS OF GREEN PLANTS THAT GROW THERE.

MONARCH REDDISH BROWN COLOR. CATERPILLAR EATS MILK-WEED.

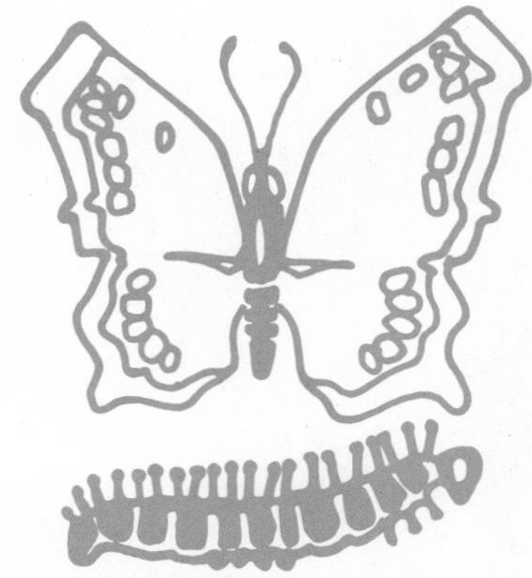

MOURNING CLOAK
DARK BROWN WITH BLUE AND YELLOW. CATERPILLAR EATS WILLOW.

TIGER SWALLOWTAIL
YELLOW WITH BLACK MARKINGS. CATERPILLAR EATS WILD CHERRY LEAVES.

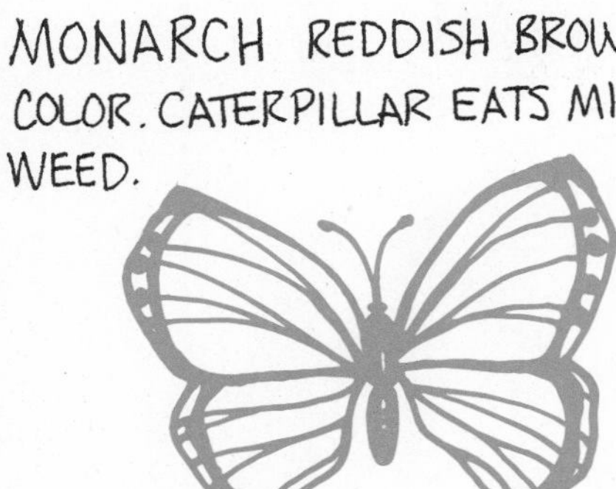

COMMON BLUE
PALE BLUE TO BROWN COLOR. CATERPILLAR EATS DOGWOOD AND CLOVER.

CABBAGE BUTTERFLY
WHITE WITH DARK PATCHES. CATERPILLAR EATS CABBAGE.

FRITILLARY
GOLDEN BROWN COLOR. CATERPILLAR EATS VIOLET LEAVES.

COULD YOU PLANT A VACANT LOT WITH PLANTS TO ATTRACT BUTTERFLIES?

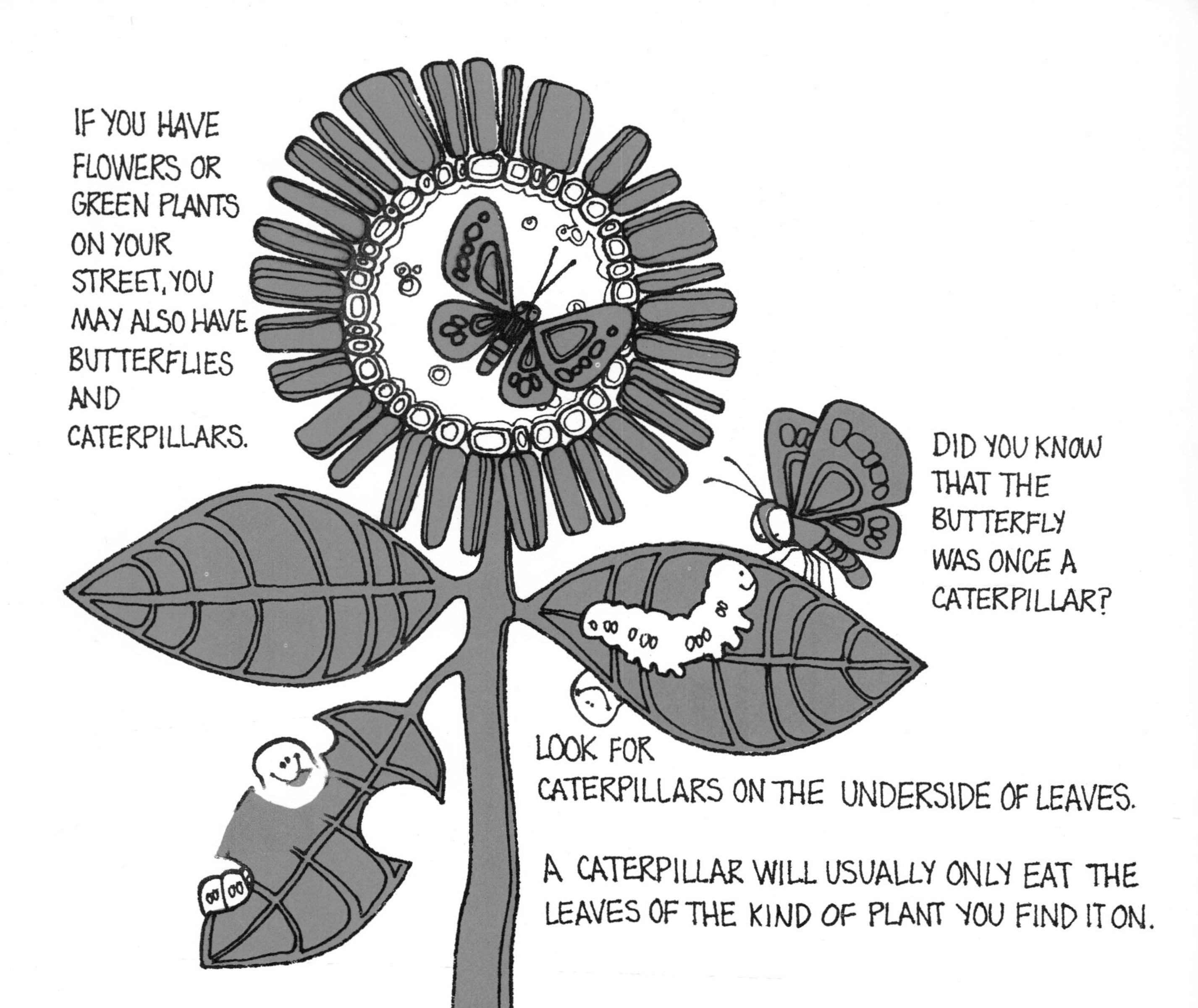

IF YOU HAVE FLOWERS OR GREEN PLANTS ON YOUR STREET, YOU MAY ALSO HAVE BUTTERFLIES AND CATERPILLARS.

DID YOU KNOW THAT THE BUTTERFLY WAS ONCE A CATERPILLAR?

LOOK FOR CATERPILLARS ON THE UNDERSIDE OF LEAVES.

A CATERPILLAR WILL USUALLY ONLY EAT THE LEAVES OF THE KIND OF PLANT YOU FIND IT ON.

IF YOU FIND A CATERPILLAR AND WANT TO OBSERVE IT, PUT IT IN A JAR WITH SOME LEAVES FROM THE PLANT THAT YOU FOUND IT ON. PUT SOME GAUZE OVER THE JAR OPENING. A RUBBER BAND WILL HOLD THE GAUZE IN PLACE.

WATCH YOUR CATERPILLAR. GIVE IT A FRESH LEAF OR TWO EVERY DAY. BE SURE TO CLEAN OUT THE CATERPILLAR'S WASTES AND DEAD LEAVES EVERY TIME YOU FEED IT.

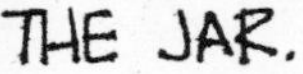

IN A FEW DAYS YOUR CATERPILLAR WILL SPIN A LADDER AND CLIMB TO THE TOP OF THE JAR.

THEN IT WILL SPIN A LITTLE PAD AND HANG DOWN FROM IT BY ITS FEET. BY THE NEXT DAY IT WILL CHANGE INTO A BEAUTIFUL CHRYSALIS. DO NOT OPEN THE JAR AGAIN UNTIL THE BUTTERFLY COMES OUT OF THE CHRYSALIS. IN A WEEK OR TWO THE CHRYSALIS WILL SPLIT OPEN AND THE BUTTERFLY WILL COME OUT.

IMPORTANT: DO NOT TOUCH THE BUTTERFLY FOR TWELVE HOURS. THEN LET IT GO.

BIRD-WATCHING IS FUN

YOU CAN BIRD-WATCH WITH YOUR BEST FRIEND, ALONE, INDOORS, IN A CITY LOT, ALMOST ANYWHERE.
BY WATCHING BIRDS, YOU CAN SEE HOW THEY FIT INTO FOOD CHAINS, HOW IMPORTANT THEY ARE TO THE ENVIRONMENT, AND HOW TO PROTECT THEM.
PEOPLE IN THE AUDUBON SOCIETY OR OTHER BIRD CLUBS ARE GLAD TO HELP NEW BIRD WATCHERS.
THERE ARE LOTS OF BOOKS THAT CAN HELP YOU, TOO.
TRY THESE PAPERBACK BOOKS: "GOLDEN NATURE BOOK ON BIRDS" AND PETERSON'S "HOW TO KNOW THE BIRDS".

WHAT DO YOU SUPPOSE BIRDS LOOK FOR WHEN THEY "PEOPLE-WATCH"?

TO IDENTIFY BIRDS, YOU NEED TO KNOW WHAT TO LOOK FOR.

CLUES TO IDENTIFICATION

WHAT **SIZE** IS IT? AS BIG AS A PIGEON? SMALLER THAN A SPARROW? ABOUT THE SAME AS A ROBIN?

WHAT **COLOR** IS IT? WHAT ARE ITS **MARKINGS**?

JAY

WHAT DOES IT **SOUND** LIKE?

BLACKBIRDS

WHAT IS THE **HABITAT**?

WREN

WHAT IS THE **SHAPE** OF ITS BILL? FEET? CREST? TAIL? WINGS?

WOODPECKER

WHAT IS IT DOING? DESCRIBE THE **ACTION**.

WHERE ARE YOU SEEING IT, AND **WHEN**?
SOME BIRDS LIVE IN ONE PLACE ALL YEAR. SOME MIGRATE.
(YOU WILL SEE THEM ONLY PART OF THE YEAR, OR AS THEY FLY THROUGH YOUR TOWN.)

FEEDING BIRDS IN WINTER

AN EASY WAY TO OBSERVE BIRDS IS AT A WINDOW STATION. MAKE ONE BY TACKING A LARGE BOARD TO YOUR WINDOWSILL. BUILD UP THE EDGE TO KEEP THE FOOD FROM BLOWING AWAY.

IF YOU PLAN TO FEED BIRDS, YOU MUST DO IT ALL WINTER LONG AND UNTIL THE BIRDS' NATURAL FOOD IS AVAILABLE AGAIN.

WHEN YOU PUT OUT FOOD FOR BIRDS, YOU MUST EXPECT OTHER HUNGRY ANIMALS TO COME. WHAT WILL YOU FEED THEM?

WHY NOT PLANT VACANT LOTS, ALLEYS, AND PLAY AREAS WITH FOOD FOR BIRDS?

HONEYSUCKLE
HOLLY
PYRACANTHA
CEDAR
FRUITS
SUNFLOWER

THE SHRUBBERY IN YOUR YARD MAY BE A NATURAL FEEDING STATION IF IT IS COVERED WITH BERRIES OR SEEDS.

DRILL HOLES INTO A LOG AND FILL THEM WITH MELTED SUET AND PEANUTS OR SEEDS.
← STOCKING MADE FROM ONION BAG FOR SUET
TACK A PIECE OF SCREENING TO BOARD TO HOLD AN EAR OF CORN.
DON'T FORGET TO SCATTER SEEDS AND CRACKED CORN UNDER THE SHRUBBERY FOR THE GROUND-FEEDING BIRDS.

HOW DOES A PLANT GROW?

ASK YOUR MOTHER FOR SOME DRY BEANS- LIMA BEANS, RED KIDNEY BEANS, OR OTHERS.
THEN SOAK SOME PAPER TOWELS IN WATER AND PACK THEM INTO A SMALL GLASS JAR. STICK THE BEAN SEEDS IN AROUND THE EDGE OF THE JAR SO YOU CAN WATCH THEM GROW. WET THE PAPER TOWELS EVERY DAY SO THEY STAY MOIST. TAKE ONE OF THE SEEDS OUT IN A DAY OR TWO AND SEE IF YOU CAN SPLIT IT OPEN. DO YOU SEE A TINY PLANT INSIDE? THE REST OF THE SEED IS FOOD FOR THE PLANT. WHICH WAY DO THE ROOTS GROW? DOES IT MATTER WHICH WAY YOU PUT THE SEEDS IN THE JAR?
WHAT IS THE BEST ENVIRONMENT FOR YOUR NEW PLANTS? PLANT THEM IN DIRT AFTER THEY GROW OUT OF THE JAR.

ARE YOU BEING
BURIED UNDER
YOUR OWN TRASH?

GARBAGE GARDENING

SAVE SEEDS FROM APPLES, ORANGES, WATERMELONS, CANTALOUPES, GRAPEFRUIT, TOMATOES, AND OTHER FRUITS AND VEGETABLES. PUT DIRT INTO THE SECTIONS OF AN EGG CARTON AND PLANT A SEED IN EACH SECTION. REMEMBER TO WATER THE SEEDS EVERY OTHER DAY.

YOU CAN GROW OTHER PARTS OF FOOD, TOO. CUT OFF THE TOPS OF CARROTS, SWEET POTATOES, AND PINEAPPLES. STICK TOOTH-PICKS INTO THE CARROT, SWEET POTATO, AND PINEAPPLE TOPS, SO THAT HALF OF THE TOP WILL SIT IN A JAR OF WATER. WHEN YOUR PLANTS HAVE ROOTS, PLANT THEM IN POTS OF DIRT.

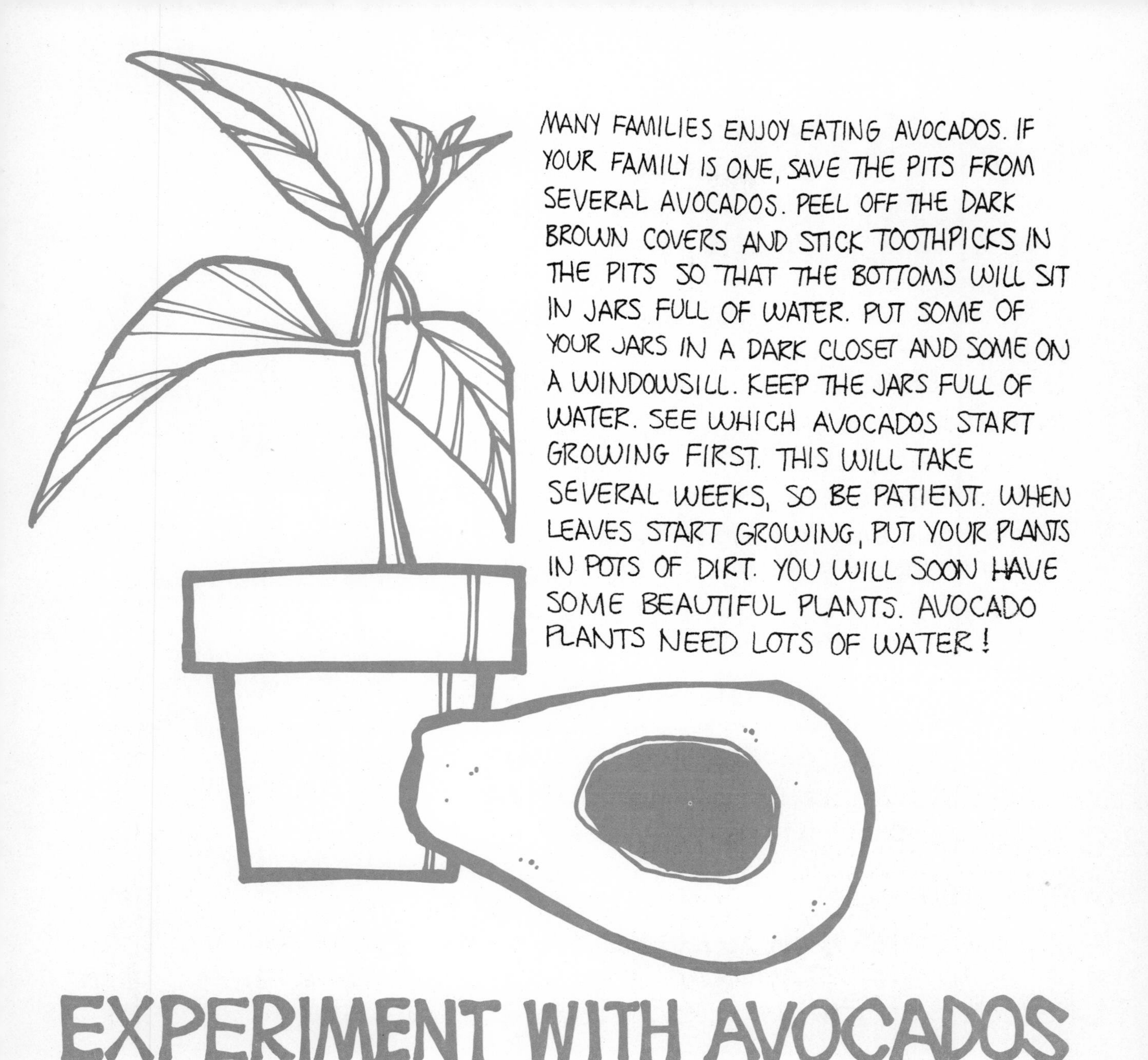

MANY FAMILIES ENJOY EATING AVOCADOS. IF YOUR FAMILY IS ONE, SAVE THE PITS FROM SEVERAL AVOCADOS. PEEL OFF THE DARK BROWN COVERS AND STICK TOOTHPICKS IN THE PITS SO THAT THE BOTTOMS WILL SIT IN JARS FULL OF WATER. PUT SOME OF YOUR JARS IN A DARK CLOSET AND SOME ON A WINDOWSILL. KEEP THE JARS FULL OF WATER. SEE WHICH AVOCADOS START GROWING FIRST. THIS WILL TAKE SEVERAL WEEKS, SO BE PATIENT. WHEN LEAVES START GROWING, PUT YOUR PLANTS IN POTS OF DIRT. YOU WILL SOON HAVE SOME BEAUTIFUL PLANTS. AVOCADO PLANTS NEED LOTS OF WATER!

EXPERIMENT WITH AVOCADOS

ONE WAY YOU CAN TELL YOUR FRIENDS ABOUT THINGS YOU HAVE DISCOVERED IS TO WRITE A POEM.

The little spider in my jar
Will never travel very far.
I think she'd rather sit and spin
A web to catch her breakfast in.

ANOTHER WAY IS TO MAKE UP A RIDDLE AND LET SOMEONE GUESS WHAT THE ANSWER IS.

DESCRIBE IT. It has feelers and it moves like a pogo stick.
TELL WHERE IT LIVES. It lives in fields and vacant lots.
TELL WHAT IT EATS. It chews up lots of plants.
TELL IF IT MAKES A SOUND. It buzzes when it jumps.

DID YOU KNOW THAT IT TAKES SEVENTEEN TREES TO MAKE A ONE-TON ROLL OF PAPER?

ASK YOUR NEWSPAPER OFFICE HOW MANY TONS OF PAPER THEY USE IN A WEEK.

SAVE YOUR PAPER. FIND OUT WHERE THERE IS A RECYCLING CENTER. TAKE YOUR PAPER THERE.

BUY RECYCLED PAPER. RECYCLED PAPER IS GOOD PAPER. LOOK FOR IT WHEN YOU BUY PAPER GOODS, BOOKS, AND MAGAZINES.

WORK AT A RECYCLING CENTER. RECYCLING CENTERS NEED HELP. MAYBE YOU CAN HELP SORT AND BUNDLE PAPER.

USE PAPER PRODUCTS OVER AND OVER.

MAKE YOUR OWN

1

TEAR ABOUT A HALF-PAGE OF A NEWSPAPER INTO VERY SMALL PIECES. PUT THEM IN A MIXING BOWL ONE-QUARTER FULL OF WATER. LET THE PAPER SOAK FOR AT LEAST ONE HOUR.

RECYCLED PAPER

7

CAREFULLY FOLD BACK THE NEWSPAPER SO YOU CAN SEE THE PULP ON THE SCREEN. LET IT DRY OVERNIGHT. THEN PEEL THE RECYCLED PAPER YOU MADE FROM THE SCREEN.

THINK OF EIGHT PAPER PRODUCTS THAT YOU HAVE USED THIS WEEK.	DRAW A PICTURE OF YOUR FAVORITE PLANT OR ANIMAL.	FIND FOUR DIFFERENT KINDS OF LEAVES.	FREE SQUARE	FIND SIX THINGS IN YOUR HOUSE THAT COULD BE RECYCLED.
FREE SQUARE	NAME FIVE PLANTS WHOSE SEEDS YOU EAT.	KNOW YOUR MAYOR'S NAME AND WHERE YOU CAN WRITE TO HIM.	FIND EIGHT THINGS IN YOUR HOUSE MADE FROM PLANT PRODUCTS.	FIND AN ANIMAL LIVING UNDER A BOARD OR ROCK.
FIND A PLANT PARTLY EATEN BY AN INSECT.	FIND A HOME THAT AN ANIMAL HAS BUILT FOR ITSELF.	FREE SQUARE	FIND A ROCK THAT IS TWO DIFFERENT COLORS.	FIND SOMETHING PRINTED ON RECYCLED PAPER.
MAKE SOMETHING FROM A TIN CAN OR A USED PAPER BAG.	FIND FIVE THINGS IN YOUR HOUSE MADE FROM ANIMAL PRODUCTS.	FIND TWO ARTICLES ON ECOLOGY IN THE NEWSPAPER.	IDENTIFY FIVE DIFFERENT BIRDS.	FREE SQUARE
FIND THREE DIFFERENT INSECTS.	FREE SQUARE	LOOK FOR TWO DIFFERENT KINDS OF CLOUDS.	FIND OUT IF THERE IS A RECYCLING CENTER IN OR NEAR YOUR CITY.	FIND THREE THINGS NEAR YOUR HOUSE THAT A BIRD COULD EAT.

vacant lotto ↓

THIS IS A GAME THAT YOU CAN PLAY ALONE OR WITH OTHERS. CROSS OUT EACH SQUARE AFTER YOU DO WHAT IT SAYS. CAN YOU CROSS OUT FIVE SQUARES IN A ROW?

ACROSS

1. EVERY LIVING THING NEEDS ____.
6. CAREFUL USE OF RESOURCES.
7. A LIVING THING THAT IS NOT AN ANIMAL.
9. A FLYING ANIMAL.
10. OUR ____ IS EVERYTHING AROUND US.
11. SOURCE OF LIGHT AND HEAT.
12. SQUIRREL FOOD.

DOWN

2. BOTH PLANTS AND ANIMALS NEED ____.
3. USE SOMETHING OVER AGAIN.
4. ________ SPOILS THE ENVIRONMENT.
5. ANIMAL AND PLANT FOOD CYCLE.
8. A CITY BIRD.

ANSWERS ON PAGE 61.

January 4

Dear Mr. Adams,

I live in your city. I see a lot of trash in the streets and it makes me mad. It looks awful. We need more trash cans. Sometimes I pick up papers, but there is no place to put them. Why don't we have more places to put litter? We really need them.

Sincerely,
Teresa West

UNHAPPY ABOUT YOUR ENVIRONMENT?

WRITE A LETTER! TELL YOUR CITY MAYOR WHAT YOU THINK. TELL WHAT BOTHERS YOU MOST. TELL WHAT YOU THINK SHOULD BE DONE. TELL WHAT YOU ARE DOING TO HELP. YOU CAN WRITE TO YOUR CONGRESSPERSON, TOO.

AND DON'T FORGET THE PRESIDENT!

WATCH FOR AIR POLLUTION, OVER-PACKAGING, NON-RETURNABLE BOTTLES, LITTER, WATER POLLUTION, AND NOISE.

ANSWERS TO CROSSWORD PUZZLE

ACROSS
1. WATER
6. CONSERVATION
7. PLANT
9. BIRD
10. ENVIRONMENT
11. SUN
12. NUT

DOWN
2. AIR
3. RECYCLE
4. POLLUTION
5. FOOD CHAIN
8. PIGEON

FOR MORE ECOLOGY FUN, READ THESE BOOKS. IF YOUR LIBRARY DOES NOT HAVE THEM, ASK THE LIBRARIAN TO ORDER THEM, OR TO SHOW YOU BOOKS LIKE THESE.

THE WORLD AROUND US

ABC OF ECOLOGY BY HARRY MILGROM. NEW YORK: MACMILLAN, 1972

BACKYARD SAFARI BY JOHN AND CATHLEEN POLGREEN. GARDEN CITY, N.Y.: DOUBLEDAY, 1971

CLEAN AIR, SPARKLING WATER BY DOROTHY SHUTTLESWORTH. GARDEN CITY, N.Y.: DOUBLEDAY, 1968

LET'S TRY IT (CATALOG NO. 19-1975, 35¢) GIRL SCOUTS OF THE U.S.A., 830 THIRD AVENUE, NEW YORK, N.Y. 10022, 1967

THIS IS A RIVER: EXPLORING AN ECOSYSTEM BY LAURENCE PRINGLE. NEW YORK: MACMILLAN, 1972

WHAT WE FIND WHEN WE LOOK UNDER ROCKS BY FRANCES BEHNKE. NEW YORK: MC GRAW-HILL, 1971

BOOKS TO ENJOY AND SHARE

ALL UPON A STONE BY JEAN C. GEORGE. NEW YORK: T.Y. CROWELL, 1971

POETRY OF EARTH BY ADRIENNE ADAMS. NEW YORK: SCRIBNER'S, 1972

THE PROCESSING AND RECOVERY OF JON THOMAS, COOL CAT. (STOCK NO. 5502·0084) AND THERE LIVED A WICKED DRAGON (STOCK NO. 0·498·439) U.S. ENVIRONMENTAL PROTECTION AGENCY. SUPT. OF DOCUMENTS, U.S. GOVERNMENT PRINTING OFFICE, WASHINGTON, D.C. 20402

THE SCROOBIOUS PIP BY EDWARD LEAR AND OGDEN NASH. NEW YORK: HARPER & ROW, 1968

CITY LIVING

ABOUT GARBAGE AND STUFF BY ANN ZANE SHANKS. NEW YORK: VIKING, 1973

BLACKOUT: NO LIGHTS FOR BRIGHTSVILLE BY LETTA SHATZ. CHICAGO: FOLLETT, 1965

CITY LOTS: LIVING THINGS IN VACANT SPOTS BY PHYLLIS S. BUSCH. NEW YORK: WORLD, 1970

COCKROACHES BY JOANNA COLE. NEW YORK: WILLIAM MORROW, 1971

LET'S LOOK UNDER THE CITY BY HERMAN AND NINA SCHNEIDER. NEW YORK: WILLIAM R. SCOTT, 1954

LIVING THINGS AND THEIR HABITAT

AT HOME IN ITS HABITAT: ANIMAL NEIGHBORHOODS BY PHYLLIS S. BUSCH. NEW YORK: WORLD, 1970

BIRDS IN THE STREETS: THE CITY PIGEON BOOK BY WINIFRED AND CECIL LUBELL. NEW YORK: PARENTS' MAGAZINE PRESS, 1971

FISH DO THE STRANGEST THINGS BY LEONORA AND ARTHUR HORNBLOW. NEW YORK: RANDOM HOUSE, 1966

SYMBIOSIS: A BOOK OF UNUSUAL FRIENDSHIPS BY JOSE ARUEGO. NEW YORK: SCRIBNER'S, 1970

WHO LIVES AT THE SEASHORE BY GLENN O. BLOUGH. NEW YORK: MC GRAW-HILL, 1962

THERE ARE LOTS OF PEOPLE WHO CAN HELP YOU FIND OUT ABOUT YOUR ENVIRONMENT. LOOK FOR THEM IN YOUR LOCAL AUDUBON, NATURE, OR GARDEN CLUB. TALK TO TEACHERS AND LIBRARIANS. TAKE YOUR QUESTIONS AND IDEAS TO PEOPLE WHO WORK IN PARKS AND MUSEUMS, OR FOR THE FOREST SERVICE.

HERE ARE SOME GOOD MAGAZINES TO READ:

CURIOUS NATURALIST
MASSACHUSETTS AUDUBON SOCIETY
SOUTH GREAT ROAD
LINCOLN, MASS. 01773 ($2.50 A YEAR)

ECO NEWS
ENVIRONMENTAL ACTION COALITION
235 EAST 49TH STREET
NEW YORK, N.Y. 10017 ($2.00 A YEAR)

RANGER RICK
NATIONAL WILDLIFE FEDERATION
1412 16TH STREET N.W.
WASHINGTON, D.C. 20036 ($6.00 A YEAR)

THE BROWNIE READER
GIRL SCOUTS OF THE U.S.A.
830 THIRD AVENUE
NEW YORK, N.Y. 10022 ($2.00 A YEAR)

YOUNG NATURALIST
FEDERATION OF ONTARIO NATURALISTS
1262 DON MILLS ROAD
DON MILLS, ONTARIO, CANADA ($3.00 A YEAR)

THESE PEOPLE SELL INEXPENSIVE BUTTERFLY-RAISING KITS:

DUKE DOWNEY
P.O. BOX 558
SHERIDAN, WYO. 82801

THE BUTTERFLY FARM
c/o CALVIN MYERS
119 CHERRY HILL ROAD
PARSIPPANY, N.Y. 07054

AUDUBON AIDS IN NATURAL SCIENCE
(A CATALOG)
NATIONAL AUDUBON SOCIETY
950 THIRD AVENUE
NEW YORK, N.Y. 10022

PROGRAM 1/74